A JIGSAW JONES MYSTERY

The Case of the
Smelly Sneaker

A JIGSAW JONES MYSTERY

The Case of the Smelly Sneaker

by James Preller

illustrated by Jamie Smith
cover illustration by R. W. Alley

FEIWEL AND FRIENDS
New York

A Feiwel and Friends Book

An imprint of Macmillan Publishing Group, LLC

175 Fifth Avenue, New York, NY 10010

Our books may be purchased in bulk for promotional, educational, or business
use. Please contact your local bookseller or the Macmillan Corporate and
Premium Sales Department at (800) 221-7945 ext. 5442 or by e-mail at
MacmillanSpecialMarkets@macmillan.com.

Library of Congress Cataloging-in-Publication Data is available.

ISBN 978-1-250-11080-0 (paperback) / ISBN 978-1-250-11079-4 (ebook)

Book design by Véronique Lefèvre Sweet

Illustrations by Jamie Smith

Feiwel and Friends logo designed by Filomena Tuosto

First Feiwel and Friends Edition—2017

Originally published as *The Case of the Sneaker Sneak* by Scholastic in 2001

Art used with permission from Scholastic

1 3 5 7 9 10 8 6 4 2

mackids.com

This book begins with a scene based on a memory,
so I dedicate it to a place, Wantagh, Long Island,
my childhood home.

Contents

Chapter 1

Splaaaaatt!

Eddie Becker grabbed my football jersey. "Okay, Jigsaw. This is it. Tie score," he urged. "If they score a touchdown now, we lose the game. You know what's coming, don't you?"

"Yeah," I grimaced. "Bigs Maloney, right up the middle."

Joey Pignattano squeezed his eyes shut. Joey didn't want any part of tackling Bigs Maloney. I didn't blame him. We'd been trying to bring down Bigs all afternoon. It was like trying to tackle a refrigerator.

Ouch. Even my bruises had bruises.

I was so black-and-blue, I looked like a grape. I'd had enough football to last me through the winter—and it wasn't even Thanksgiving yet.

Bobby Solofsky clapped his hands together. He shouted, "All right, let's win this game!" Solofsky was quarterback for the other team. He stood over the ball. Ralphie

Jordan got set, waiting for Bobby to hike the ball. Ralphie was playing wide receiver. He was faster than a text.

Joey Pignattano, my teammate, lined up opposite Ralphie. "You wouldn't hurt a guy with glasses," Joey bleated.

I stood across from Bigs Maloney. It was my job to cover Bigs. After all, no one else wanted to do it. Bobby called out the signals,

"Ready, set, green thirty-nine! Blue twenty-six! Orange-orange, green-green. Hut-one, hut-two, hut-threee . . ."

"Oh, just hike the ball already," Eddie complained.

I glanced warily at Bigs. No, smoke didn't pour from his nostrils. Horns didn't grow from his head. And Bigs didn't wear a ring through his nose. But in every other way, Bigs resembled a bull in a rodeo, busting to break loose. He was getting the ball, all right. I knew it. He knew it. Everybody on the planet knew it. I bet even the little green men on Mars knew it.

Bigs Maloney was going to take the ball, and he was going to run right over me.

And like a rubber dummy, I was going to try to stop him. I knew something else, too. In about ten seconds, I was going to be flatter than a tortilla at Taco Bell.

Who invented football, anyway?

"HIKE!" Bobby yelled.

Ralphie sprinted down the sidelines, arms waving. "I'm open! I'm open!"

Bobby faked a pass to Ralphie.

"Watch out for the Quarterback Sneak!" Eddie called out.

Suddenly, Bigs circled back and took the handoff from Bobby. It was the Statue of Liberty play! Bigs wrapped two thick arms around the ball. He cradled it to his

belly. Bigs pawed the ground, snorted, and charged.

Where was a red cape when I needed one?

Aaaaaaargh!

Whap, kersplish, oof, splaaaaatt!

The next thing I knew I was lying flat on my back. Dizzy, I stared at the spinning sky. A few clouds floated past. They were white and fluffy. One even looked like a wittle, itty-bitty bunny wabbit. Off in the distance—far, far away—I heard Bigs Maloney rumble into the end zone. Or maybe it was a herd of rhinos tap-dancing on my skull. I wasn't sure.

Joey knelt beside me. He poked at me with his finger. "Jigsaw? Are you okay?"

I blinked. At least my eyelids weren't broken. "Anybody get the license plate of that marching band? I think I was just trampled by a tuba."

"Don't try to talk, Jigsaw," Joey said. "You're not making sense."

Ralphie and Bigs gathered around me. "S-s-sorry, Jigsaw," Bigs stammered. "I didn't

mean to hurt you. It's just that you were sorta in my way. Do you think you can walk?"

"Sure I can walk," I muttered. "You put one foot in front of the other."

"Can you get up?"

"Don't be silly, Bigs," I said. "Of course I can. But right now I'm doing my impression of highway roadkill. I'm pretending to be a chicken who tried to cross the road at the Daytona 500. What do you think?"

Ralphie whistled softly. "I think you look like the agony of defeat."

"I think you look like road pizza," Bobby observed.

"I think you need a hand," Joey said. He reached down to help me up. And that was all anybody needed to know about Joey Pignattano. He'll help you up when you're feeling down.

Chapter 2

The Challenge

After a few minutes, the feeling returned to my hands and feet. "Hey, look." I pointed. "Here comes Helen, Lucy, and Danika."

We walked over to check out their scooters. That is, everybody else walked. I limped. "Cool scooter," Joey complimented Helen Zuckerman. "Can I try it?"

"Yes . . ." Helen answered, "if you let us play football."

"Sure, why not!" Joey answered.

"*Why not?!*" Bobby repeated. "WHY

NOT??!! I'll give you a good reason why not. Take a look at 'em, Joey. They're girls."

"So?" Joey replied.

"Girls can't play football," Bobby stated. "It's un-American."

"Oh, yeah?" Danika Starling challenged.

"Yeah."

"Can too."

"Can't."

"Can."

"Can't."

Eddie stepped between Danika and Bobby. "This is fascinating, guys," he cracked. "But Sunday night is pizza night at my house. And I'm never late for pizza. I'll see you all in school tomorrow."

Bobby slid his tongue across his teeth. He made a sucking sound with his mouth. That was Solofsky for you. My dog, Rags, had better manners. "Consider yourself lucky we didn't let you play," Bobby said to Helen.

"Girls can't play football. Everybody knows that."

Helen's cheeks flushed with anger. Lucy Hiller's eyes burned. Danika put her hands on her hips in defiance. "Girls are just as good as boys," Lucy seethed.

"Maybe better," Danika added.

Bobby laughed in slow motion.

Like this: Ha. Ha. Ha. Ha.

"What's so funny, Solofsky?" Helen said. "You afraid we might beat you?"

Bobby rolled his eyes skyward. "Afraid of you? That's a good one." A devilish grin crept across Bobby's face. "Bigs, Ralphie, and me just beat Eddie, Jigsaw, and Joey. I bet the three of us could beat any four girls in a game of football."

The girls huddled together, talking with hushed voices. Finally, Helen spoke up. "You're on," she said. "Name the time and place."

"Tuesday after school. Right here in the field behind the playground. That way you'll have a day to practice," Bobby quipped. "You'll need it."

"We've still got to find a fourth player," Helen said.

"A fourth *victim*, you mean," Solofsky replied. "Just make sure it's a girl. Any girl you want."

Ralphie and Bigs watched all this in silence, scratching their heads. It didn't look like they loved Bobby's idea. But it was too late. The game was set.

"One more thing," Danika said. "We'll need a referee. Someone we can trust."

"What's the matter? You don't trust me?" Bobby asked.

"I'd rather trust a rattlesnake," Lucy retorted.

"What about Jigsaw?" Joey suggested. "He's honest."

Helen Zuckerman glanced doubtfully at me. "Jigsaw . . . *and Mila*, together. A boy *and* a girl. I'll call Mila as soon as I get home."

My ears perked up. Mila Yeh was my best friend. She was also my partner. We solved mysteries together. Now, I figured, we worked football games, too.

Helen reached out a hand to Bobby. "Deal?"

"Deal."

They shook on it.

"Tuesday," Helen confirmed. "Two days before Thanksgiving. Right here. Girls against boys."

"Just like the Super Bowl," Ralphie joked. "We'll call it the Turkey Bowl!"

Helen, Danika, and Lucy hopped on their scooters. They sped away without looking back.

Bobby let out a whoop. He smiled happily. "We'll kill 'em!" he shouted. "It'll be *sooooo* easy." He paused to look at Bigs and Ralphie. They weren't smiling. "What's the matter, guys? It'll be like taking candy from a baby."

"I guess," Bigs mumbled. "But I sort of like babies."

"And four against three," Ralphie said. "I don't know."

"Oh, stop your whining!" Bobby said. "They're *just girls*. We'll destroy 'em!"

"One last thing," Bobby added, jabbing a thumb in my direction. "Jigsaw, you're the hotshot detective. Keep an eye on those girls. I don't want 'em to try any tricky stuff. Us guys have to stick together."

I had to bite my lip not to laugh out loud. Solofsky was the world's biggest cheater. It was like a wolf telling me he didn't trust sheep!

Chapter 3

The Spring Street Superstar

I took a long bath after dinner. Soaking my bones in the warm water, I decided that the next time I tried to tackle Bigs Maloney, *I wouldn't.*

I worked on a jigsaw puzzle until bedtime. That's how I got my nickname, Jigsaw. Because I love piecing together puzzles. My real name is Theodore. But only my mom still calls me Theodore. Everybody else knows me as Jigsaw.

I solve mysteries like I solve puzzles. One piece at a time.

Most nights my dad reads to me, or I read to him. Sometimes we take turns. That night, we read two chapters in *Skinnybones* by Barbara Park. Then my dad tucked me in and turned out the light. "Don't let the bedbugs bite," he chimed. I yawned, closed my eyes, and pretended to sleep. After he left, I pulled out my flashlight. I had other plans. I grabbed my trusty detective journal and a marker.

I wrote a secret message in code. It was called a Ticktacktoe Code. It's sort of like

making your own secret alphabet. This is
the letter key:

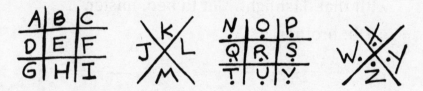

The alphabet for the code comes from the
letter key like this:

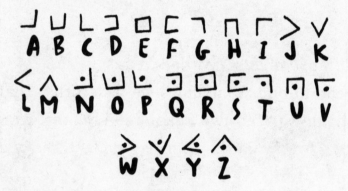

I jotted down a quick note to Mila.
There was a sudden rapping at my door.

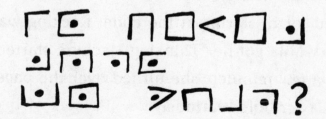

"Theodore Andrew Jones," my mother's voice called. "You're not fooling anybody with that flashlight. Get to bed, mister."

Oh, brother.

First thing Monday morning, I handed the note to Mila on the bus. Mila rocked back and forth, staring at the code. Rocking was how Mila got her Thinking Machine started. In a few minutes, she turned over the page. Mila scribbled furiously:

"I don't get it," I said. "Do you really think Helen's team can win?"

"I know we can," Mila replied.

I raised an eyebrow. "*We?* Don't tell me you are going to play on Helen's team."

"Nope."

"Who, then?" I asked. "Athena? Geetha? Kim?"

Mila shook her head. "Nope, double-nope, triple-nope."

"Tell me," I demanded.

"Sorry, Jigsaw. It's a secret. But I will tell you this. I'm the coach!"

"What?!" I exclaimed. "I thought you were going to referee with me!"

"Geetha Nair will do it instead." Mila's expression turned serious. "You've got to understand, Jigsaw. This isn't an ordinary football game. The girls against the boys. I'm going to help Helen's team win."

"No one on Helen's team can tackle Bigs Maloney," I warned. "Believe me, he'll trample 'em like a steamroller."

Mila shook her head. "We've got a secret weapon."

The bus turned onto Spring Street. We stopped in front of Helen Zuckerman's house. Helen's older sister, Lydia, boarded the bus after Helen. Lydia Zuckerman was a playground legend at our school. She was tall and talented and tough as nails. Nobody messed with Lydia Zuckerman.

When she walked down the aisle to her seat in the back of the bus, Lydia gave Mila a sly nod.

"See you at practice," Mila said.

Lydia grunted. I took that as a yes. Two grunts, I guessed, meant no.

"Lydia Zuckerman!" I whispered to Mila. "The Spring Street Superstar?! She's the best athlete in our whole school. I can't believe you got her to play for you!"

Mila's eyes twinkled with delight. "Don't tell anyone," Mila said. "It's our little secret."

I crossed my fingers behind my back. "Sure," I lied. Maybe lying wasn't a nice thing to do. But like Mila said, this wasn't an ordinary football game.

Chapter 4

Doing the Turkey Lurkey

I found Bobby, Ralphie, and Bigs talking in the hallway.

Solofsky didn't even blink when I told him the bad news. "Big deal," he bragged. "We'll still destroy 'em."

Ralphie and Bigs exchanged worried glances.

"She's a legend," I said. "Lydia Zuckerman is the fastest kid in school. She's strong, too. My brother Nicholas is in her class, and he says she beat everyone in an arm wrestle."

"I don't believe it," scoffed Bobby. "Boys rule. Girls drool. We'll win the game, easy."

He turned to Ralphie and Bigs. "Right?"

"Er, yeah, right," they answered.

It was a busy school day. Thanksgiving was just three days away. Our teacher, Ms. Gleason, read a really good book called *The Perfect Thanksgiving* by Eileen Spinelli. Ms. Gleason was really funny when she read it. We got a little crazy, laughing and rolling around on the floor. Loving books was contagious in our classroom. It was catchy, sort of like the time when Stringbean Noonan started sneezing and our whole class got sick. *The Perfect Thanksgiving* showed how two different families celebrated Thanksgiving. One family was quiet and tidy. The other was loud and messy. They reminded me of Thanksgiving at my house. But no matter how different the families were, Thanksgiving meant the same thing to both of them. It was a day to be thankful. A day to celebrate our love for each other.

Plus, of course, we get to eat pie!

All our classwork had something to do with turkeys—even in math and science. Ms. Gleason helped us compare tame turkeys to wild turkeys. We made a big chart and hung it on the wall:

TAME TURKEYS	WILD TURKEYS
1) live on a farm	1) live in woods
2) fat and slow	2) slim and quick
3) can't fly	3) fly up to 50 mph
4) short necks	4) long necks
5) short legs	5) long legs
6) not so bright	6) very smart and cunning

"I'd much rather be a wild turkey than a tame one," Stringbean Noonan concluded.

Ms. Gleason agreed. "Me, too. *Especially* during Thanksgiving!"

No one could argue with that. We all knew what happened to turkeys on Thanksgiving. And it wasn't pretty.

Gobble-gobble . . . GACK!

"Can anyone tell me what bird is our national bird?" Ms. Gleason asked.

About ten hands shot to the sky. "Oh, oh, oooooh! Ms. Gleason! Ms. Gleason!!"

Ms. Gleason called on Joey. But Joey just

stared into space. "I think I used to know when I raised my hand, Ms. Gleason," Joey admitted. "But now I sort of completely forgot."

Ms. Gleason covered a smile with her hand. "How about you, Kim? Do you sort of remember?"

"A bald eagle," Kim Lewis answered.

"That's correct," Ms. Gleason said. "But here's an interesting fact. Benjamin Franklin wanted another bird to be our national bird. He preferred the wild turkey! What do you kids think?"

We discussed different birds. Geetha liked owls. Bobby voted for the vulture. Lucy admired seagulls. But most of us stuck with the good old American bald eagle.

"Poor baldy," Ralphie joked. "Too bad we can't buy him a wig!"

Everybody laughed.

Ms. Gleason glanced out the window. It

was raining hard. "It looks like we won't be going outside for recess today. So let's take an exercise break. Stand up, everyone."

She told us that wild turkeys follow a set pattern when they scratch the dirt. A pattern is when the same thing happens over and over again. We studied patterns in math.

"I call this dance the Turkey Lurkey," Ms. Gleason announced.

She tucked her arms to her sides. She gave the floor a long scratch with her left foot. Then two quick scratches with her right foot. Then another with her left foot. Soon, everybody was wandering around the room, gobbling and scratching, stretching their necks and flapping their wings.

That's when our principal, Mr. Rogers, stopped by.

Uh-oh.

"What's going on here?" he demanded.

We froze in place.

Ms. Gleason laughed. "It's the Turkey Lurkey!" she announced. "Please join us, Mr. Rogers! The children will show you how!"

Mr. Rogers sighed heavily, shook his head sadly, and eyed the door hopefully.

"PLEASE!" a chorus of voices chimed.

Flap, flap. Scratch. Gobble.

"Come on, Mr. Rogers," Kim Lewis said. "You can do better than that!"

And Kim was right. After a while, Mr. Rogers scratched and flapped with the rest of us. I've got to hand it to him. After a little practice, Mr. Rogers made a pretty good turkey! He'd better be careful next time he goes to the supermarket. Some hungry shopper might take him home and pour gravy on his head!

Chapter 5

Swiped!

I thought I'd be watching the Turkey Bowl on Tuesday afternoon. Instead I was tackling a mystery. Somebody had swiped Bigs Maloney's smelly sneakers.

It was 1:45. We had just gotten back from the library. Ms. Gleason was on the reading rug, gabbing to a group of kids. They were trying to write a play about Squanto, the Native American who helped the Pilgrims.

I was sitting at my table with Bigs, Lucy, and Stringbean Noonan. I drew a picture of a steamroller crushing a football player.

I labeled the steamroller BIGS. I drew an arrow at the frightened football player. It read, THE GIRLS' TEAM.

Who says art is only for sensitive types?

Lucy leaned forward and gave Bigs a friendly tap. She teased, "Are you ready to lose today?"

"I'm ready to *win*," Bigs replied, smiling broadly. He gestured toward the cubbies. "I've got my football sneakers in my backpack right over . . ."

The smile fell from his face and crashed to the floor. "My backpack?!" he roared. "It was right on that hook. Where'd it go?"

We found the backpack on the floor near the front door. The zipper was open. It was empty, except for a few rocks. "My sneakers are gone!" Bigs scowled. "They've been stolen!"

A group of kids gathered around. Everyone felt bad for Bigs. Except Helen. She was only worried about the game. "No sneakers, huh?" Helen said. "Tough break, Bigs. But like they say on Broadway, the game must go on."

Bigs gestured to his heavy hiking boots. "I can't play in these clunkers!"

"He's right," Bobby protested. "The game's called off. Our best player can't play in boots."

Helen howled. "Called off? No way! Find someone else to take his place. Stringbean is wearing sneakers. He can play."

We turned to look at Stringbean Noonan.

Stringbean shook his head from side to side. "Nuh-uh," he said, his eyes wide and full of fear. "I'm allergic to football. It gives me a rash."

We didn't call him Stringbean for nothing. Jasper Noonan was the skinniest kid in room 201. Sure, he was smart and friendly and all that good stuff. But Stringbean couldn't tackle a cupcake. I'd hate to see him tangle with Lydia Zuckerman.

"We'll play *tomorrow*," Bobby promised. "Right, Bigs? You've got another pair of sneakers at home, don't you?"

"I want my best pair," Bigs stated, arms crossed. He turned to me. "Looks like you've got a mystery to solve, Jigsaw. No game until you find my sneakers."

I held out my hand. "You know our rates, Bigs. A dollar a day, plus expenses."

"But . . ." Bigs stammered.

"But me no buts," I said. "No money, no detective work. You do the math."

Bigs reached into his pocket, peeled off a dollar, and handed it to me. Bigs didn't seem too happy about it—like George Washington was his best buddy. He hated to say good-bye.

Mila pulled Bigs aside. "Can you remember the last time you saw your sneakers?" she asked.

"I don't want to talk about it," Bigs said.

"Do you want us to find your sneakers or not?" I challenged.

Bigs thought for a moment. "It was after recess," he finally said. "I remember

because I found some dinosaur fossils in the playground. I put them in my backpack when we came inside."

"*Fossils?*" I asked.

Bigs shrugged. "Okay, okay. Just rocks, probably. But they looked cool."

His story made sense. If you found a cool rock, you kept it forever. Or until your mom made you throw it away.

"You wanted to *keep* a rock?" Mila asked. She seemed confused. "Why?"

"It's a guy thing," I explained.

"Oh, like burping," Mila noted.

"Exactly."

"Recess was right before library," I reminded Bigs. "Are you *sure* that's when you last saw your sneakers?"

"Sure I'm sure," he stated.

I reasoned, "Somebody must have sneaked in when we were at the library. It's the only time the sneakers could have been taken."

"I guess," Bigs mumbled.

"One thing's for sure," I told him. "We're looking for a sneaky sneaker thief."

I scribbled in my detective journal:

CLIENT: BIGS MALONEY.

THE CASE OF THE SMELLY SNEAKER

"Hmmm," Mila said, pulling on her long hair. "I just had an idea. Follow me, Jigsaw."

Chapter 6

The Kid in the Hall

Mila pointed down the hall. "There he is, George Seaver."

"Good thinking, Mila. Maybe George saw something."

George Seaver was a playground legend. He was the biggest troublemaker in school. Nearly every day his teacher, Mrs. Koosman, made George sit out in the hall. She even kept a desk out there for him.

George had a way of making her batty. I'm sure George's pet python, Fang, didn't help.

To this day, Mrs. Koosman refuses to open desk drawers.

George was drawing a picture and giggling to himself. Without looking up, he said, "Jigsaw, Mila. What's what?"

"More like who's who," I said. "We're working on a case. We're wondering if you might have seen anything."

George finished the picture. It showed a boy flying happily above the clouds. I looked closer. The boy in the picture looked exactly like George. He shoved the page under a stack of papers.

"What are you drawing, George?" Mila inquired.

"Comics," George replied. "I'm going to publish graphic novels someday."

"But in the meantime," I added, "you'll be happy making Mrs. Koosman bonkers."

George smiled devilishly. "Hey, it's a living."

I told George about the case. Yes, he told us, he was out in the hall at that time. And, yes, he did see a few people go into the room.

"Who?" Mila asked.

George opened his palm. "The question is: *How much*?"

"This better be worth it," I said, and dropped two quarters into George's hand. George pocketed the change. "Let's see. Short girl, curly hair, red boots."

"Lucy Hiller," Mila concluded.

"That creepy Solofsky kid," George continued, making a disapproving face. "Mr. Copabianco, the janitor. He emptied the trash."

"Anyone else?"

George nodded. "Yeah, that girl who wins all the trophies. What do they call her? The Spring Street Superstar."

"Lydia Zuckerman?" I asked. "Are you sure?"

"That's the one. No doubt about it," George said.

We thanked him and returned to class.

Ms. Gleason called us over to her desk. "What are you two up to?"

I leaned close. "We're working on a case."

Ms. Gleason put down her blue pencil. "Oh, my. Is it very, very dangerous?"

I nodded.

If Lydia Zuckerman had anything to do with this, it could be very, very dangerous indeed. But that's life when you're a detective. Danger is the name of the game.

When the bell rang at the end of the day, we all headed for our buses. In the lobby,

I heard Nicole Rodriguez call out, "Wrong way, Lucy! The bus is out here."

"My mom's picking me up today," Lucy told her. "I have to wait here. We're going shopping at the mall!"

I noticed Bigs and Ralphie. They were standing just inside the front doors.

"Come on, guys. We'll miss our bus," I said.

"Not today," Bigs explained. "My mom is taking us to Gump's Roller Mania. She's leaving the twins with a sitter."

Ralphie smiled.

"Oh," I said. "Sounds like fun. See you around."

I slowly walked to the bus.

I guess you can't get invited to everything.

Mila smacked me on the shoulder. "Cheer up, Jigsaw," she said. "We've got a mystery to solve."

Chapter 7

The List of Suspects

Mila came over after school. We did our homework right away. Then we went down to my basement office.

My dad was already down there. He was messing around in his workshop.

"What are you doing home?" I asked.

"I live here. Remember?" he replied.

"I mean, why aren't you at work?"

He smiled. "My ducks."

"Your ducks?"

"Yes," he replied. He gestured to a couple

of wooden ducks on his workbench. "Crested grouse, actually. They were calling my name. So I took the day off," he explained.

Mila looked to me for answers.

"What can I say?" I told her. "It's his hobby. He likes carving wooden ducks. Go figure."

"We'll be in my office," I said. My dad nodded, then picked up a paintbrush. He whistled softly to himself.

Like my brother Billy said, "Dad's a little *quackers*."

Mila and I talked about the case. We tried to answer all the "W" questions—when, where, what, why, and who. We already knew *when*, *where*, and *what*. But we were still working on *why* and *who*. I wrote a list of suspects in my journal. Each one had been seen going into room 201 at the time of the crime.

SUSPECTS
Lucy Hiller
Bobby Solofsky
Lydia Zuckerman

"What about Mr. Copabianco?" Mila asked.

"Mr. Copabianco was just doing his job," I replied. "He always gets the trash in the afternoon. Besides, why would he want Bigs Maloney's sneakers?"

"Yeah, *why*," Mila murmured. "That's the big question."

"*Why* is easy. The thief wanted Bigs out of the game," I reasoned. "Bigs couldn't play without his sneakers. You heard Helen. She wanted the boys to use Stringbean Noonan instead. That would have given her team a fighting chance."

I circled Lydia Zuckerman's name. "Suspect number one," I said.

"I think Bobby did it," Mila suggested.

"Bobby? Why would he steal from his own teammate?" I asked.

"Look at what happened next," Mila argued. "When the sneakers turned up missing, Bobby canceled the game."

"He had no choice," I said.

"He was afraid of losing," Mila declared.

"That's crazy," I said. "Bobby has been bragging about the Turkey Bowl nonstop."

"Exactly," Mila replied. "If the boys lost, he'd look foolish."

"Tell you what," I said. "You check out Bobby and Lucy. I'll pay a visit to Lydia Zuckerman. I want to know what she was doing in room 201."

"Be careful," Mila warned. "Lydia's no pushover."

"Neither am I," I said.

I yawned, long and slow, as if the idea of confronting Lydia Zuckerman wasn't worth worrying about.

If I was nervous, nobody had to know.

Chapter 8

Lydia

Helen Zuckerman opened the front door. "Jigsaw!" she squealed. "What are you doing at my house?"

"I'm here on business," I stated. "A little matter of stolen sneakers. Is your sister home?"

"Lydia?" Helen asked in surprise.

I dug my hands into my pockets. "You got another sister I don't know about?"

Helen led me into what she called "the exercise room." I heard Lydia's grunts and groans from behind the door. "Thirty-six . . . thirty-seven . . . thirty-eight . . ."

The place was a regular gymnasium. There was a weight set on the far wall. An exercise bike. A rowing machine. The works. Lydia was on a floor mat, doing sit-ups. She wore sweatpants and a T-shirt with the sleeves cut off.

"Not now," Lydia said.

"I've only got a few questions," I offered.

"I'm busy," Lydia retorted.

Lydia grabbed a towel and ran it across her face. She started on a set of push-ups.

I stood beside her, arms on my hips. "I don't want trouble," I said. "But a witness saw you at the scene of a crime. I'm not leaving until you give me answers."

"What crime?" Lydia grunted.

"Bigs Maloney's sneakers took a walk," I told her. "Thing is, Bigs's feet weren't in them at the time."

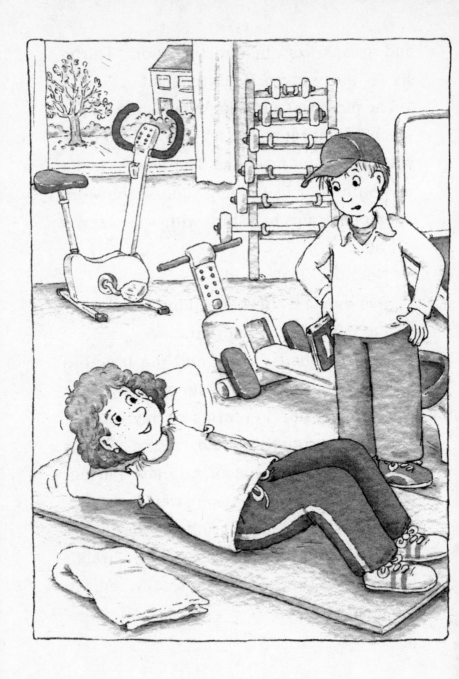

Lydia sighed and slowly rose. I stood my ground. Lydia glared at me. She leaned forward then blew into my face, like I was a birthday candle. I didn't flinch. Lydia laughed softly. "You've got guts, Jones."

Lydia grabbed a hand weight. "You talk. I'll lift."

I checked my detective journal. "Our witness says you were in room 201 at around one-thirty," I said. "Is that true?"

"I was delivering interschool mail," she answered. "There was a letter for Ms. Gleason."

"Can you prove it?"

"You're the detective—*you* prove it," Lydia snapped. "All I know is I put an envelope in Ms. Gleason's in-box."

"Too bad about the Turkey Bowl," I said.

"It's all the same to me," Lydia commented. "I was planning on a football game today. No game, that's okay, too. I'll get my exercise one way or another."

I turned to leave.

Lydia looked me up and down. "Hey, detective. You ever think about exercising?"

"I tried lifting weights once," I answered. "But they were too heavy."

Lydia smiled. "You're funny, Jones."

"Yeah, a regular laugh riot," I mumbled. I shut the door behind me.

Walking home, I thought it over. I was certain that Lydia was telling the truth. The letter to Ms. Gleason would be easy enough to check.

Then it hit me. I remembered Lydia's words: "*I was planning on a football game.*"

She was planning on it.

I thought of my old pal Ralphie.

He had different plans.

So did Bigs Maloney.

And so did Lucy Hiller.

All three of them had plans.

Only none of their plans included football.

Chapter 9

The Confession

"May I be excused?" I asked at dinner.

"So soon?" my mother asked. "Don't you want dessert?"

"No, thanks," I said.

My mother felt my forehead. "Are you feeling ill?"

I pushed back my chair. "It's not that, Mom. I've got business to take care of."

I called Mila from the hallway. "I think Ralphie and Bigs are in on this together," I said. "Lucy might be involved, too."

"Go on," Mila said. "I'm listening."

I continued. "Remember after school? Ralphie and Bigs had plans to go roller-skating."

The silence lasted a few moments. Then Mila suddenly gasped, "I get it! They already knew there wasn't going to be a football game!"

"Very good, detective," I said. "They knew the Turkey Bowl would be canceled. They even planned on it."

Mila added, "Lucy had plans to go to the mall."

"Bull's-eye," I said. "You win the rubber chicken. But how did they do it?"

"It could have been Lucy," Mila suggested. "Lucy told me she went back to room 201 to get an overdue library book she'd left in her cubby."

"And Bobby?" I asked.

"That's the funny thing," Mila said. "He went back at the same time as Lucy. They were in room 201 together."

"Bobby and Lucy together," I murmured. "Meet me at Ralphie's house. Let's get to the bottom of this."

Mila was already in Ralphie's room when I arrived. We'd been there plenty of times before. It had dark paneling and the roof sloped in sharp angles. It felt like a cozy little cave.

Like Bigs Maloney on the football field, I decided to plow right up the middle. Only the name of my game was crime-busting. "You're hiding something," I told Ralphie. "You *knew* there wouldn't be a game today."

"But . . ."

I cut him short. "No buts, Ralphie. No tall tales. Just give me the truth."

Ralphie stared at me. He was deciding which way to go. Or maybe he was trying to think of a good lie. Finally, he just smiled.

"Bigs and Lucy were in on it, too," Ralphie confessed. "We never wanted to play that game in the first place. Don't get me wrong. I love football. But I want it to be fun. With Helen and Bobby, it was like, um, a war or something."

Mila and I exchanged glances.

"I was the last one out of the classroom when we went to the library," Ralphie explained. "It was my job to turn out the lights. After everyone left, I took the sneakers from Bigs Maloney's backpack. I hid them in the trash can."

"The trash can?" Mila repeated. "Why?"

"We needed Lucy to be involved, too," Ralphie said. "She's a girl. That way it wouldn't be like the boys were scared or anything. It was the boys and girls together, you know. Lucy didn't want to play, either. She was supposed to smuggle the sneakers out of room 201."

"*Supposed to?*" I echoed. "Didn't Lucy do it?"

"She *tried*," Ralphie said. "But I think Bobby knew something was up. He followed Lucy into the classroom. She never had a chance."

"Imagine that," I mused. "Bobby Solofsky helped *prevent* a crime. That's a first."

"Where are the sneakers now?" Mila asked.

Ralphie picked at the sleeve of his sweater. "That's what worries me," he admitted. "They're still in the trash."

"Does Bigs know?" I asked.

Ralphie shook his head. "He thinks Lucy's got 'em."

I chewed it over, like a dog with a big bone. "Okay," I said. "It's time for Operation Rescue."

Chapter 10

To the Dumpster

Beep-beep. BEEP!

My brother Billy leaned on the horn. Ralphie Jordan zoomed down his porch steps. He squeezed into the backseat with Lucy and Mila.

"Thanks again," I told my brother. "It's nice of you to give us a ride to school so early."

Billy rubbed his tired eyes. "I still don't understand why you couldn't take the bus."

I heard Lucy whisper nervously from the backseat, "I hope we're not too late."

We had to beg Mr. Copabianco at first. Finally, he let us into the school. We told him it was an emergency. Normally, kids aren't allowed into the school until 9:00 a.m.

"I'll walk down with you," he said cheerfully. "Let's make this snippy-snappy. I've got work to do."

He took out a large key ring. He selected a key, put it into the lock, and turned. As soon as the door opened, Lucy rushed forward. She raced to the trash can. "It's empty!" she cried.

Ralphie was crushed.

"Uh-oh," Mila said. "This means trouble."

"Not just trouble," Ralphie groaned. "*Bigs* trouble."

Mr. Copabianco stood in the doorway. He rubbed his chin thoughtfully. "They don't empty themselves, you know."

I turned and stared at good old Mr. Copabianco. His mouth formed a sly smile beneath his mustache.

"Where do you put the trash?" I asked.

"Into a bigger garbage can," Mr. Copabianco said. "Then it goes to the dump."

"THE DUMP!" Lucy exclaimed. "We're doomed!"

"Not so fast, Lucy." I suddenly remembered the dumpster behind the school. Once a week a large garbage truck picked up the trash.

"What day is the dumpster emptied?" I asked.

Mr. Copabianco looked at his wristwatch. "Why, should be any minute," he said.

"Quick!" I screamed. "To the dumpster! And thanks, Mr. Copabianco. Thanks a lot!"

Chapter 11

Touchdown!

Lucy Hiller held her nose. "Bleck!"

Ralphie made a face. "You want us to climb into that thing?"

"Don't look at me," I said. "I didn't steal the sneakers. I'm not swimming in that slop."

Mila giggled.

Lucy stared up at the dumpster, scratching her head.

"Do you need a boost?" I snickered.

"Stop smiling," Lucy complained. "This isn't a joke. It's . . . it's . . ."

"Gross?" Mila offered.

"Disgusting?" I suggested.

"It's the pits!" Ralphie lamented. He sighed, then slowly climbed into the dumpster. Lucy followed behind, still holding her nose.

"The sneakers are in there somewhere," I said. "Just dive right in."

"Ugh," Lucy whined. "It smells like something died in here."

"Nah," I said. "That's just yesterday's hot lunch special. Be careful you don't step on any Swedish meatballs."

Suddenly, a voice boomed, "Hey, HEY! You crazy kids!! Get out of there!!!"

It was Mr. Copabianco. He was running toward us, waving his arms. "What on earth are you children thinking?" he demanded.

We told him what on earth we were thinking.

He listened carefully. Then laughed, long and loud.

"Why didn't you just ask?" he bellowed. "I found those sneakers yesterday! I knew it must be a mistake. Nobody throws away perfectly good shoes. I've already returned them to Ms. Gleason's room. Didn't you notice them on her desk?"

We found Bigs Maloney's sneakers back in room 201. They were right where Mr. Copabianco said they'd be. Sitting behind a stack of books . . . on the corner of Ms. Gleason's desk . . . about five feet from her empty trash can.

Whoops.

We decided to play the Turkey Bowl early on Thanksgiving morning.

"But just for fun," Ralphie insisted.

Bobby and Helen reluctantly agreed.

"And the boys and girls get mixed up together," Lucy said. She smiled sweetly at Bigs. "I want to be on your team, *Charlie*."

Lucy was the only person on the planet who called Bigs by his real name. The big lug turned purple with embarrassment.

The game was a blast. Lots of people played, including my brothers Daniel and Nick, my sister, Hillary, and a bunch of neighborhood kids.

Even a few parents joined us.

"Football on Thanksgiving," my father said. "It's an American tradition, like fireworks on the Fourth of July."

Lydia Zuckerman caught the opening kickoff. She raced to the left sideline, then suddenly reversed direction. Twisting and turning, she darted and faked. No one

touched her. You couldn't help but stand back and admire her talent.

Lydia raced into the end zone. She spiked the ball into the ground. Touchdown!

Everyone cheered—even players on the other team. It didn't matter. We were all playing ball together. Having fun.

Just playing a game.

After a while, we forgot to keep score.

Because in the end, only one score mattered.

Jigsaw Jones: One.

Mysteries: Zero!

The Case from
Outer Space

When **Joey** and **Danika** find a mysterious note
tucked inside a book, all signs point to a visitor
from outer space. Yikes! Can Jigsaw solve this
case, when the clues are out of this world?

A Knock on the Door

Call me Jones.

Jigsaw Jones, private eye.

I solve mysteries. For a dollar a day, I make problems go away. I've found stolen bicycles, lost jewelry, and missing parakeets. I've even tangled with dancing ghosts and haunted scarecrows.

Mysteries can happen anywhere, at any time. One thing I've learned in this business is that anyone is a suspect. That includes friends, family, and a little green man from outer space.

Go figure.

It was a lazy Sunday morning. Outside my window, it looked like a nice spring day. The sky was blue with wispy clouds that looked like they had been painted by an artist. A swell day for a ball game. Or a mystery. Maybe both if I got lucky.

I was standing at my dining room table, staring at a 500-piece jigsaw puzzle. It was supposed to be a picture of our solar system. The sun and eight planets. But right now it was a mess. Scattered pieces lay everywhere. I scratched my head and munched on a blueberry Pop-Tart. Not too hot, not too cold. *Just right.* As a cook, I'm pretty good with a toaster. I began working on the border, grouping all the pieces that had a flat edge. Sooner or later, I'd work my way through the planets. The rust red of Mars. The rings of Saturn. And the green tint of Neptune. I've never met a puzzle I couldn't

solve. That's because I know the secret. The simple trick? Don't give up.

Don't ever give up.

My dog, Rags, leaped at the door. He barked and barked. A minute later, the doorbell rang. *Ding-a-ling, ding-dong.* That's the thing about Rags. He's faster than a doorbell. People have been coming to our house all his life. But for my dog, it's always the most exciting thing that ever happened.

Every single time.

"Get the door, Worm," my brother Billy said. He was sprawled on the couch, reading a book. Teenagers, yeesh.

"Why me?" I complained.

"Because I'm not doing it."

Billy kept reading.

Rags kept barking.

And the doorbell kept ringing.

Somebody was in a hurry.

I opened the door. Joey Pignattano and Danika Starling were standing on my stoop.

We were in the same class together, room 201, with Ms. Gleason.

"Hey, Jigsaw!" Danika waved. She bounced on her toes. The bright beads in her hair clicked and clacked.

"Boy, am I glad to see you!" Joey exclaimed. He burst into the room. "Got any water?"

"I would invite you inside, Joey," I said, "but you beat me to it."

Danika smiled.

"I ate half a bag of Jolly Ranchers this morning," Joey announced. "Now my tongue feels super weird!"

"That's not good for your teeth," I said.

Joey looked worried. "My tongue isn't good for my teeth? Are you sure? They both live inside my mouth."

"Never mind," I said.

"Pipe down, guys!" Billy complained. "I'm reading here."

"Come into the kitchen," I told Joey and Danika. "We'll get fewer complaints. Besides, I've got grape juice. It's on the house."

"On the house?" Joey asked. "Is it safe?"

I blinked. "What?"

"You keep grape juice on your roof?" Joey asked.

Danika gave Joey a friendly shove. "Jigsaw said 'on the house.' He means it's free, Joey," she said, laughing.

Joey pushed back his glasses with an index finger. "Free? In that case, I'll take a big glass."

Chapter 2

One Small Problem

I poured three glasses of grape juice.

"Got any snacks?" Joey asked. "Cookies? Chips? Corn dogs? Crackers?"

"Corn dogs?" I repeated. "Seriously?"

"Oh, they are delicious," Joey said. "I ate six yesterday. Or was that last week? I forget."

Danika shook her head and giggled. Joey always made her laugh.

I set out a bowl of chips.

Joey pounced like a football player on a

fumble. He was a skinny guy, but he ate like a rhinoceros.

"So what's up?" I asked.

"We found a note," Danika began.

"Aliens are coming," Joey interrupted. He chomped on a fistful of potato chips.

I waited for Joey to stop chewing. It took a while. *Hum-dee-dum, dee-dum-dum.* I finally asked, "What do you mean, aliens?"

"Aliens, Jigsaw!" he exclaimed. "Little green men from Mars—from the stars—from outer space!"

Thank you for reading this **FEIWEL AND FRIENDS** book.

The Friends who made

The Case of the
Smelly Sneaker

possible are:

Jean Feiwel, Publisher

Liz Szabla, Associate Publisher

Rich Deas, Senior Creative Director

Holly West, Editor

Alexei Esikoff, Senior Managing Editor

Raymond Ernesto Colón, Senior Production Manager

Anna Roberto, Editor

Christine Barcellona, Editor

Kat Brzozowski, Editor

Emily Settle, Administrative Assistant

Anna Poon, Assistant Editor

Follow us on Facebook or visit us online at mackids.com.

OUR BOOKS ARE FRIENDS FOR LIFE.